Herbster Readers

SAYING "THANK YOU"

Written by Cecilia Minden and Joanne Meier • Illustrated by Bob Ostrom
Created by Herbie J. Thorpe

ABOUT THE AUTHORS

Cecilia Minden, PhD, is the former director of the Language and Literacy Program at the Harvard Graduate School of Education. She is now a reading consultant for school and library publications. She earned her PhD in reading education from the University of Virginia. Cecilia and her husband, Dave Cupp, live outside Chapel Hill, North Carolina. They enjoy sharing their love of reading with their grandchildren, Chelsea and Qadir.

Joanne Meier, PhD, has worked as an elementary school teacher, university professor, and researcher. She earned her BA in early childhood education from the University of South Carolina, and her MEd and PhD in education from the University of Virginia. She currently works as a literacy consultant for schools and private organizations. Joanne lives in Virginia with her husband Eric, daughters Kella and Erin, two cats, and a gerbil.

ABOUT THE ILLUSTRATOR

Bob Ostrom has been illustrating children's books for nearly twenty years. A graduate of the New England School of Art & Design at Suffolk University, Bob has worked for such companies as Disney, Nickelodeon, and Cartoon Network. He lives in North Carolina with his wife Melissa and three children, Will, Charlie, and Mae.

ABOUT THE SERIES CREATOR

Herbie J. Thorpe had long envisioned a beginning-readers' series about a fun, energetic bear with a big imagination. Herbie is a book lover and an avid supporter of libraries and the role they play in fostering the love of reading. He consults with librarians and matches them with the perfect books for their students and patrons. He lives in Louisiana with his wife Misty and their daughter Carson.

The Child's World

Published in the United States of America by The Child's World®
1980 Lookout Drive • Mankato, MN 56003-1705
800-599-READ • www.childsworld.com

Acknowledgments
The Child's World®: Mary Berendes, Publishing Director
The Design Lab: Kathleen Petelinsek, Design;
Gregory Lindholm, Page Production
Assistant colorist: Richard Carbajal

Library of Congress Cataloging-in-Publication Data
Minden, Cecilia.
  Saying "thank you" / Cecilia Minden and Joanne Meier ;
illustrated by Bob Ostrom.
    p. cm. — (Herbster readers)
  Summary: "A simple story belonging to the second level
of Herbster Readers, young Herbie wonders how best to show
his family members his appreciation for all they do."—Provided
by publisher
  ISBN 978-1-60253-016-4 (library bound : alk. paper)
  [1. Behavior—Fiction. 2. Bears—Fiction.] I. Meier, Joanne D. II.
Ostrom, Bob, ill. III. Title.
  PZ7.M6539Say 2008
  [E]—dc22   2008002594

Herbie Bear loves his family.

He wants to show them with a special *Thank You*.

But how?

"I know!" said Herbie.

"I can bake Mom a batch of *Thank You* brownies."

"I can put a *Thank You* shine on Dad's shoes."

"I can give Hannah a big bunch of *Thank You* flowers."

"I can give Hank's teddy bear a *Thank You* wash."

"I can paint Grandpa's fence with a bright *Thank You* color."

"What can I do for Grandma?"
thought Herbie.

21

Grandma baked his favorite peanut-butter cookies.

Herbie decided to give Grandma's best china a *Thank You* scrub.

"Herbie," said Grandma,
"Do you know what I would like?"

"The best *Thank You* of all. . .

. . . a Herbie-Bear hug!"